Ma Dear's
Old Green House

by Denise Lewis Patrick
illustrated by Sonia Lynn Sadler

Library of Congress Cataloging-in-Publication Data is available.

Published by Just Us Books, Inc.
356 Glenwood Avenue
East Orange, NJ 07017
www.justusbooks.com

10 9 8 7 6 5 4 3 2 1
Printed in Hong Kong
First Edition

Lots of things are green,
like lizards and leaves and
those big sour pickles
that drip all over your hands.

My grandma, Ma Dear, had a green house.
Ma's old house, the house we visited
in summertime, was very green.

Ma's porch was perfect
for playing checkers, being "It"
in hide-and-seek,
or just watching cars crawl by.

And it was the best place
to eat messy watermelons
with lots of salt
seeing who could spit seeds
the farthest.

Or even learning to
ride your bike,
I thought.

But when I flew right off
the porch's edge,
getting up full of scrapes
and tears,
I knew that was
a mistake.

It was better to lay
in cool damp grass under the tall pecan tree,
counting four leaf clovers.

It was better still to race around the house, squealing until some grown-up yelled, "Y'all hush up!"

So we'd run in panting quietness, grabbing fat figs
from the backyard trees, sending chickens
flying to their coops, making the noise
we weren't allowed.

And inside the green house was a television shaped like a brown box that had gray, white, black people moving on the screen. We huddled around it, waiting to sing along, waiting to laugh along.

Inside, Ma had a tall china closet
that she locked with a key.
It was not from China but it held cups
that were made in Japan, along with
fancy and forgotten stuff
that we could stare at, not touch.

We wondered who ever did.

The refrigerator was in the dining room,
which left plenty of space in the kitchen
for Sunday morning hot biscuits,
all buttery and oozing grape jelly.

Church clothes
were always in danger.

And the big mystery was that there was no bathtub in the bathroom! Ma never told us why, only warmed water on her kitchen stove...

...to fill a round tub for our evening baths.
At night Ma always dunked an elbow,
making sure it was just right before we hopped in.
Before we sailed across the world in our tin tub boat.

After, we cuddled in Auntie Fran's bed
under quilts older than we were,
quilts made of colored cloth wheels
that used to live as our mothers'
shirts and skirts and dresses.

We wiggled and the colored wheels rolled
across our cold toes, warming them.

We whispered all night long.

We whispered, then slept
between dreams and crowing roosters
'til morning sun crept in,

until that new day's sun started shining
in Ma's old green house.

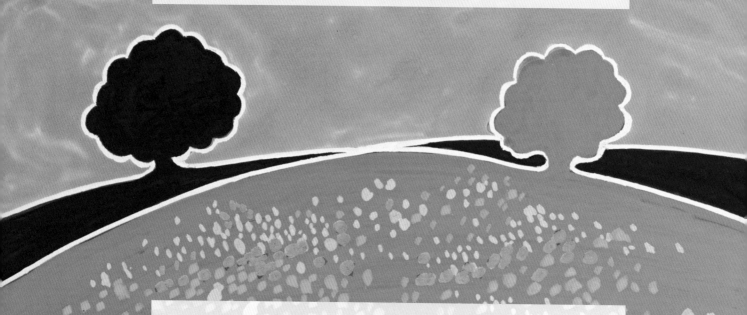

Lots of things change between summers.
One year during the in-between time,
my grandma got a new house.

We didn't understand why the tin tub
and out-of-place refrigerator had to go,
but Ma told us, "Sometimes grandmas
need new things. All grandmas like nice
things, especially houses."

So the old house was torn down
and a new one was built on the very
same spot.

It does not have a porch.
It's not even green.

But it's so good that some things stay the same,
like lizards and leaves and that pecan tree
in Ma's old yard.

When we drive up we can see.

That pecan tree keeps growing taller,
just like we do.
And it remembers summers
at Ma Dear's old green house,
just like we do.

About the Author

Denise Lewis Patrick comes from a storytelling family. Her father wrote poetry, and she followed in his footsteps, penning her first writings at eight years old. A native of Natchitoches, Louisiana, she earned a B.A. in Journalism from Northwestern State University, then moved to New York City to begin her professional writing career. She has since written over 25 books for children including *Red Dancing Shoes* and *Martin's Friendship Lesson*. Denise took inspiration for her most recent book, *Ma Dear's Old Green House* from childhood summers filled with cousins, fun and her grandmother's old green house in Louisiana. Now grown-up, Denise lives in New Jersey with her husband and their four sons in a green house of her own.

About the Illustrator

Sonia Lynn Sadler was born at Fort Riley, an army base in Kansas. She studied fine arts, illustration and crafts at Maryland Institute College of Art, and went on to graduate from Parsons School of Design in New York City. After a successful career in design working for such companies as Anne Klein, and Liz Claiborne, Sonia launched www.SoniaLynnSadlerArts.com, where she markets her artwork and accessories. Her unique scratchboard and acrylic paintings are widely exhibited in galleries across the country. *Ma Dear's Old Green House*, is her first trade picture book for children. Sonia's home and studio are located in northern New Jersey.

Cover and Layout Design by Stephan Hudson 2nd Chapter